JACK CAFE BECOMES A GREAT INVENTOR

MONOSIJ MITRA

Part 3 Jack Café becomes a great inventor

I had landed on a dark cave. I had gone to F2L planet from this cave. I had just touch back side of the torch. The touch switch was on. I had successfully came out of the cave with great difficulty. I was very happy to see my sister. I know everything about my sister but my dad told me to pretend of knowing nothing. Alice said, "Jack! It had been around fourteen years since I had met you." I asked, "Alice! How are you?" She replied, "I am fine. How did you get this torch?"

I replied, "I got this torch from F2L planet." I had touch the back side of the torch. The light that was coming from the torch got disappear. A man voice came, "Wow! This torch working system is to advance." I had stared at the man and asked, "Are you, my brother-in-law?" The man said, "Yes. My full name is Jonathan wells and I lived in Las Vegas." I asked him, "What's your occupation?" He said, "I am a hotel manager in a 5 stars hotel." I asked Jonathan, "What's the name of the hotel?"

He replied, "Bellagio Las Vegas Hotel." I said to Alice, "Let us go home. What is today's date?" Alice replied, "Today's date is 22nd June 2028. Your birthday is on 19th September." I nodded my head. Alice took out her phone. I said to her, "Boroko can help us to reached the sea beach." Alice replied, "Jack you are right. For fourteen years US government did a lot of research in this island. Google had developed a translating device that can help us to communicate with the tribal people.

We proceeded our way towards the tribe colony. Few people saw us proceeding towards the tribe colony. They gave us a sign to wait here. We were few hundred meters away of entering tribe colony. After sometime Boroko had come to see us. He immediately recognized me and gave us a welcoming gesture. Alice asked in the translating device, "Boroko can you help us in reaching to the sea beach?" Boroko nodded his head. We followed him and had safely reached to the sea beach.

A ship was waiting for us. The captain of the ship proceeded towards us. He said, "Jack, welcome to my ship." I asked him, "What is your name?" He replied, "I am captain Kiefer and I live in Germany. Where do you lived?" I replied, "I lived in Washington." We had talk for some time and finally we had entered the ship. This island was situated at 30.631-degree north latitude and 65.89-degree west longitude. My house was 1370 kilometer away from this island. We had went to our ship room. I had asked Alice, "What is the time?" She saw the time in her phone and told me, "Now it 5 PM. Would you like to see the sunset?" I nodded my head.

Within two days we had reached our home. In these two days I had seen the sun rise and the sun set. The ship was completely empty. This ship had a small restaurant inside it. We used to have our breakfast, lunch and dinner in that restaurant. I had pressed the door calling bell. My mom had opened the door. She said to me, "It's been years since I had seen you." I replied, "Mom, I miss you so much." We went inside our home. We kept our shoe inside a shoe rack. My dad said, "I have two bad news for you. Your grandfather had pass away nine years ago. Your grandmother had pass away five years ago."

Everyone had a sad face and I had went to the washroom for changing my dress. After changing my dress, I asked my dad, "Will I be continuing my education?" My dad replied, "I want you should be home school." I replied, "In future I will give entrance exam for high school." My dad said, "After two years you will be giving your entrance for high school. Your teacher will prepare you for the entrance exam. Will you be staying here or with your sister?"

I replied, "I will be staying with my mom and dad." My parents were very happy about it. Jonathan said, "We are returning after two days." I asked my mom, "When did we shift from our old apartment?" My mom replied, "We had change our apartment after your grandmother death. Tomorrow nine in the morning your teacher will come." That day I went to sleep at 10 PM and woke up at 7 AM. Before 9 AM I was completely ready for my class.

I heard a calling bell at 9 AM. My sister had opened the door. The woman who was standing outside said, "I am Sophia Dottie." Alice asked her, "Are you Jack new teacher?" She nodded her head. Alice said, "Please welcome to our home." She entered to our home. My dad called me. I had come out of my room to see dad. I had finally saw my new teacher. She said, "Jack, I am Sophia." I replied, "Good morning, ma'am." She said, "Good morning, Jack. When you went to F2L planet I was studying in 6th grade."

My dad had told everything about me to her. My first day went quite nice with her. She gave me 5th grade final paper to solve in front of her. The paper was 50 marks. She gave me 90 minutes to solve the paper. I was able to solve the paper on time. I said to Sophia ma'am, "I had completed the paper." She replied, "You had completed the paper five minutes before the schedule time. Let me correct your paper." She corrected my paper. She said to me, "You are genius. You got full marks without any sort of revision."

On 9th July I had completed 5th grade all subject final question paper. So far Sophia ma'am had taught me only two hour a day after each subject exam. She gave me a month to prepare for 6th grade final paper. She had provided me the material to study. She said to my father, "Mr. Café I will not be coming for a month. Jack needs to prepare for 6th grade final paper." In my dream I got enough time to prepare for my exam. On 9th August I heard a calling bell at 3 PM. I had opened the door and saw Sophia ma'am.

I said to Sophia ma'am, "Good afternoon, ma'am" She wished me back. She removed her slippers out and entered in. She went to my room, followed by me. I had made my study table ready for the exam. I had received a math paper from her. The paper was for 100 marks. I was able to complete the paper within the schedule time. Sophia ma'am said, "A Day after tomorrow you will be getting your marks." She went away from my home. Alice asked me, "How was your exam?" I replied to her, "I had answered all the question correctly."

Alice showed me a thump up. She later shared my words to other people. On 11th August she came to my home. As usual she went to my study room. She said to me, "You had scored full marks in math." She later conveyed this same information to my parents. I had written science exam today. I had written the exam well. Before living my home Sophia ma'am said, "On 13th August you will have your next exam but I won't say the name of subject."

On 13th August I had heard a calling bell. Dad had opened the door. Sophia ma'am every time came at 3 PM. I was waiting for her in my room. She entered my room and said, "Wow you are genius! I did not inform you that last exam was science. It is possible to manage math but not science. I am confuse to know your strength and weakness. You scored 96/100 in the science exam. A normal people can score up to 90 not more than that. Today I will give you literature."

I had receive the literature paper from Sophia ma'am. I had completed the paper within the schedule time. I had submitted the paper to Sophia ma'am. She collected the paper from me and said, "Your next paper is on 15th August. All the best for your next exam." I replied to her, "Thank you ma'am." On 15th August I heard a calling bell. I had opened the door to greet Sophia ma'am. We had went to the study table. Sophia ma'am said, "In literature you had scored 95/100. Today you will write 100 marks of Grammar and writings."

I had received the paper from her. I had completed the paper on time. I had handover the paper to Sophia ma'am. Sophia ma'am said, "On 17th August you will be writing your last test." She proceeded out of my home. On 17th August I heard a calling bell. I had welcome Sophia ma'am to come inside my home. I asked her, "Which school you use to study fourteen years ago?" She replied, "I use to study in Lakewood middle school." We went to my study room. Sophia ma'am said, "You had scored 95/100 in Grammar and Writing. Today you will have your computer practical. You will have computer practical for 100 marks. I am giving you 4 hours to complete your exam. Don't worry in case you fail the test. I did not teach you anything in computer. A normal human cannot pass this test."

I had seen a simulation of parallel universe in my dream. In my lucid dream Sophia ma'am had taught me computer. I had successfully completed the computer practical within the schedule time. Sophia ma'am said, "Please have your evening snacks." I had left the room to have my evening snacks. After having my snacks, I had return to my room. She said in surprise, "You are going to get novel prize in future. Now the whole world should see you. You scored full marks in the practical exam." I did not think about the novel prize.

She went out of the room and my mother was there. She said to my mother, "Aunty your son is genius he had scored full marks in a computer practical that was not taught by me. I would like him to come in TV." My mom had discuss this matter with my dad. My dad had contacted a news channel and they will be coming on 25th August. Everyone in my family was very excited about it. Sophia ma'am went to her home happily. The following days Sophia ma'am started teaching me class 7 potion. She was teaching me 3 subject per day.

On 25th August 2028 I heard a calling bell in evening. My dad had opened the door. Some news reporter had come. My dad had welcome them to come inside. I had come to the living room. That day Sophia ma'am was with me. They had made their set ready. One male reporter asked to me, "What is your name?" I replied to him, "I am Jack Café." He asked, "Why you are being home school?" At this point I had narrated about my journey to F2L planet. Sophia ma'am said to him, "I gave Jack grade 7 computer practical but I did not teach him. I was surprise to know that he had correctly done those problem."

The reporter asked me, "How did you correctly done the computer practical?" I replied, "I just thought out of box." He asked the audience, "Can Jack Café become a great scientist or inventor in future?" My interview finally got over. The news reporter and other people left our home. My dad told me not to reveal the secret of Lucid dreaming. I felt that my unknown soulmate must be watching the news channel. I feel to visit Plum restaurant on 27th August. This restaurant was just 2.8 kilometers away from my house.

Sophia ma'am left our home after having dinner with us. My dad said to me, "If you have not gone to F2L planet you would marry Sophia. I had seen a parallel version of you in my dream. I was the president of USA in that parallel version. On 27th August our whole family will have dinner at Plum restaurant". I asked my dad, "Why do I feel to visit this restaurant on 27th August?" My dad replied, "You will know the secret after five years." From my dad statement I came to know that I will meet my soulmate in this restaurant.

On 27th August we visited the Plum restaurant. My dad drove us to Plum restaurant. Only three of us visited it. We had our Lunch in it. We had return to our home after having lunch. The next day onwards Sophia ma'am took my regular classes. On 30th August I had visited my grandfather graveyard. This was the day when my grandfather had pass away. That day Sophia ma'am did not take my class. Next day I had resume my regular classes from Sophia ma'am. My classes were going well.

On 19th September I found a gift on my sturdy table. It was around 8 in the morning. On top of the gift happy birthday Jack was written. I had recognize the handwriting of my dad. I had recognize there was one more gift for me. I had decided to open my birthday gifts tomorrow. An hour later Alice and Jonathan had arrived. Alice and Jonathan had wish me happy birthday. They gave me birthday gifts. I had kept the gifts safely on my sturdy table. Soon we had our breakfast.

My father said, "Let us play a game. Jack will be in his room. Randomly anyone will be knocking the door and he need to guess who had knock the door. He will be writing the name as knock 1 person name. When he is done in writing a name, he will be knocking the door back.

Let us fixed the knock four times in this game." I had went inside my sturdy room and had closed the door. I heard four knocks of somebody. I had closed my eyes and it seem the sound wave strike my ears. I was able to visualize what laid outside of the door.

Alice had knock the door. I had written my answer in a sheet of paper and had knock the door thrice. Alice had opened the door. She said, "I was the one who had knock the door. Let me see your answer." She was shock to see my answer. She said, "Your guess was right but you can't guess correctly for remaining family member." Fortunately, I was able to guess all the people who had knock the door. Everyone in my home was surprise and congratulated me. In the evening Sophia ma'am had come to our home.

I had a nice birthday party. I had celebrated my Christmas vacation and new year party in Bellagio Las Vegas Hotel. Our stay in the hotel was completely free. We had return to our home on 4th January 2029. On 14th February Sophia had completed in explaining 7th Grade syllabus. I had my final exam from 1st March to 14th March. On 20th May 2029 my dad had received a phone call from Jonathan. After the conversation my dad said to us, "Good news! Alice is going to be mother. I will be organizing a party very soon in our home."

Next day he had contacted an organization who are involve in designing party. The organization had agreed to host a party on 27th June. They will charge after the completion of party. My sister and Jonathan's family was invited to join the party. I had invited some of my friends in apartment. My dad had selected a place for the party. That place was 27 kilometers away from my home. On 27th June 2029 all the invited people had come to the party. After the party we were not left with any excess food item.

Alice was shock as she was expecting to have some excess food stock. Alice asked her dad, "Dad! How is it possible to have no excess stock of food?" Dad replied to her, "You much appreciate Jack accurate calculation. He is excellent in finance, even though he had never studied finance. We had the best cake with cheapest price." Alice said, "Even a finance manager cannot do such a wonderful calculation. My brother is genius!"

On 9th January 2030 mid night I saw a strange dream. I was meditating in my dream. When I opened my eyes, I found myself sitting in meditating posture. I had awaken from my dream. How is it possible that I was sitting on my bed? Every day I had the same dream. On 19th January 2030 Sophia had completed 8th grade syllabus with me. That day she said, "Directly you will be writing entrance exam for high school." I had nodded my head.

On 10th February we started packing our luggage to go Las Vegas. The airport was 20 kilometers from my home. We left the home at 7 PM. Within half an hour we had reached the airport. We had our dinner at airport. Before 10 PM we had went inside the flight. Our flight had taken off at 10 PM. The flight had landed at 2:30 AM. I had slept between 3 to 4 hours in the flight. Within 4 AM we were out of the airport. Alice house was around 5 kilometers away from airport.

It did not take much time to find a taxi. We kept our luggage inside the taxi dickie. Within ten minutes we had reached Alice house. They had welcome us to visit their home. This was the first time I had visited my sister's house for the first time. She asked her dad, "How was your journey?" My dad replied, "We had an excellent journey." All of us had taken bath. Jonathan said to my dad, "Mr. Jackal the doctor had confirmed that the delivery needs to be done on 19th February at

6 PM." An old lady comes out of a room. Jonathan said, "My mom's name is Dannielle Johnson. She was a computer analytics. Now she is 59 years old. Last year she had taken retirement. Dad, may you come here?"

An old man comes out of a room. He said, "Jackal, nice to see you again. This your younger son. His name is Jack and I had seen him in TV. He is going to be next Nicola Tesla." I replied, "Thank you Uncle." He gave a smile to me. Dannielle asked us, "Would you people see our house?" My dad replied, "We had seen the house except Jack." She said to me, "Jack, please follow me." I had followed her to see the house. The house consisted of two rooms for guest and three rooms for other family member.

Overall, it was a 5BHK house. I asked Dannielle, "How old is this house?" She replied, "The house was built by my husband in the year 2000. His name is Jerome. He used to be a gymnast. He used to represent our country in Olympic. Our son is having an ordinary life. He did not became a celebrity like his dad. I am kind of introvert in nature. I like to talk to people in private. At the age of twenty he had done his first appearance in Olympics. He had taken his retirement in the year 2004. He had first appeared in the year 1988 in the Olympics." I had return to the living room after seeing the house.

They had some more additional room apart from three room in ground floor, two room for guest. They had three bathrooms, a theatre room, a library. On 16th February 2030 Jonathan had taken appointment with Kindred Hospital Las Vegas Sahara. Next day afternoon Alice was admitted inside the hospital. On 19th February 6 PM she had given birth to a baby boy. At that time everyone was present inside the hospital. From doctor we came to know that she will be released on 21st February.

On 21st February my nephew had first time step inside the house. On 23rd February we left their house and proceeded towards the airport. Within an hour we were done with all sort of security check up. Several minutes later we were done with our boarding pass. At 11 AM the flight had taken off and landed at 3:30 PM. We had our lunch in the plane. We had booked a taxi to reach our home. Sophia was done in training me for entrance exam.

I had decided to invent a medicine that will help anyone to lucid dream. This medicine will be in a liquid form. The name of medicine will be Ketasonide. No person should not consume more than 10 ml within an interval of two days. If someone consume 5 ml per day, they will get powers to change their dream and explore dream world easily. After a month I had arranged all the material to make the Ketasonide. I had started making the Ketasonide. I had given my entrance test after a month in Timber high school.

After a month my dad had received a phone call from Timber high school. After the phone call my dad said to me, "Congratulation! You had cleared the entrance test. I will buy you a new phone tomorrow." I replied to my dad, "I am very excited to have my first phone." Next day I had went to a mall. In the mall I found a place where they sold mobile phone. My dad had bought a phone that belong to Morito company. This phone was manufacture by Japanese company. My phone costed only 500 dollars. We had return to our home.

I had saved my mom and dad number. I had receive my sister and Jonathan numbers from my dad. Later in the evening I had called Alice. I said, "Hello." Alice replied, "Hello Jack, congratulation of having a new phone." I said, "Dad had bought me a new phone. What's my nephew's name?" She replied, "His name is George." I said, "Bye, I will call you later." I had drop my phone call. I had created a Metaverse, Instagram and Linkin. Earlier Metaverse was known as facebook.

Six years ago, the name facebook was lost and Metaverse had come into existence. In metaverse we can meet friend in a virtual world. I had decided to meet some friend in Metaverse. I found something was lacking in this virtual world. I was able to see the virtual world from my subjective reality. I had decided to first finish making my medicine. I will be keeping my medicine under preservation. I started making my medicine. My high school classes started on 1st July 2030.

On first day only I was able to remember all my classmate's name. Maybe one or two classmates knew my name. Next day when everyone came to the classroom, they were shock to know that I know all the classmate's name. My class teacher said to me, "Wow! You had excellent memory." I replied, "Thank you. Can I have access to the library?" She nodded her head. Her name was Arla Ball. She appeared to be in middle age. She was of ordinary height nor tall or short. She had a short hair.

I had a class strength of 14 girls and 16 boys. At the break time I had gone to library. I had spotted an interesting book. The book name is "The Physics of Tachyons" written by Ernst L. Wall. This was the first time I had been hearing this word. This book was 35 years old. I had completed reading this book on 10th July. On 11th July I had return the book to library. I had understand the meaning of Tachyon. Tachyon is a virtual particle that can travel faster than speed of light.

I had done a deep analysis on this particle and did not understand such particle do exist in universe. There were many other things to understand about this particle. On 25th November 2030 I had completed in inventing my medicine. I need to develop my own software before selling it to public. I had preserve the medicine in freezing temperature. On 2nd December my midterm had started. My exam got over on 16th December. My regular classes had started. That day I had started working on developing a software.

In Christmas I had visited my sister house. We had stayed in her house still 3rd January. On 6th January my school had reopen. On 21st January I had received my midterm result. In average I had scored 97 percent and was colledge topper. Towards the end of March, I had my final exam. My final exam got over on 21st March. I had receive my result on 14th May. I had scored 95 percentage in my final exam. I had completed developing my software on 16th June 2031. Three months later I had transform my ordinary smart phone into a holographic mode.

The name of my software was Tarmova. I had called my dad, "Dad would you like to see my new invention?" My dad had called my mom to see my new invention. They had arrived in my room in a short time. My mom asked, "What invention did you do?" I had shown the holographic version of my phone. My mother was shock and dad had a smile in his face. I think dad know my future. I asked my father, "Do you know my future?" He replied, "I know your future but you will not be knowing your future. It will cause disturbance in the timeline if you know future."

I said, "I am ready to face any circumstance in the future." My mom said, "Jack you are genius. I would like you to upload your invention in you tube." I had nodded my head. I had uploaded my invention on 23rd September in you tube. I had explain the working of holographic mode. In the holographic mode you can see the holographic version of people. It is up to the person to view multiple things in the holographic version. I had receive a comment from NASA CEO to share my number.

My parents were very happy to hear this news. I had shared my number with him. Next day I had receive a phone call from him. He said, "Good evening, Jack Café." I replied, "Good evening, sir." He asked me, "You studying in which grade?" I replied, "I am studying in grade 10. You are NASA CEO Omar Legg." He said, "I am impress with your intelligence. You will be doing full time work once you complete your graduation. In between in your vacation you can work here. Please give me update about your vacation well in advance."

I replied, "Yes." On 11th February 2032 I had manage to give advertisement about my medicine. I had also shared my number publicly. I had received a phone call on 23rd February 2032 from Sun Pharmaceutical industry limited. They had invited me to give a speech about my invention 28th October 2032. I had went to Sun Pharmaceutical industry limited on 28th October 2032. I had not been going to school for few days. A woman guided me to the boss cabin. The CEO of Sun Pharmaceutical industry limited was waiting for me.

I said, "It's pressure to meet MR. Everett David." Everett sir replied, "Nice to meet Jack Café. I had studied about your medicine. This medicine will bring a great revolution in our society. We are thinking of constructing your office building in Princeton New Jersey." I asked Everett, "What about my staying in Princeton New Jersey?" He replied, "The construction of your Office will be done like a bungalow. I believe you will earn 200 million dollars over a span of five years. We had created a bank account for you. We will be helping you selling your product online. I would like to give this paper for your signature."

I had gone through the paper carefully and had signed the paper. They had shown me the design of my future bungalow. I will be receiving money from my medicine sell. The paper is not fake from all angle. I told the offer to my parents after reaching home. They were very happy about my achievement. I had started selling my medicine. I had earn 23,000 dollars after a month time. My sister had given birth to a baby boy. I had been arranging everything in my own. I had also created a website for hiring people.

A week later I had receive a resume from a CPA for job. On the same day my new born nephew had been name Jefferey. I had gone through the resume and had called him for interview. Her name was Mary Morrison. I had decided to take the interview on 15th January 2033. On 15th January 2033 Mary Morrison had come for the interview. The interview will take place in my bed room. I asked her, "Mary can you sit in this chair?" She had sat on the chair facing opposite to my sturdy table.

I had taken my seat on my bed. My total income had become 41,000 dollars. I asked Mary Morrison, "Did you participate in any extra-curriculum activity?" She replied, "I had participate in theatre show, Mono acting, group drama." I asked her, "What is your weakness?" She replied, "I need to improve in singing, typing speed, painting." I asked her, "What is book keeping?" She was surprise to hear this question from me. She knows that I had not sturdy commerce or business.

She replied, "Bookkeeping is the recording of financial transactions, and is part of accounting in business and other organizations." I asked her, "What do you mean by account?" She replied, "An account is a record in an accounting system that tracks the financial activities of a specific asset, liability, equity, revenue, or expense. These records increase and decrease throughout the accounting period." I asked her, "What is goodwill?" She replied, "The goodwill is an intangible asset that associated with the purchase of one company from another."

I asked her, "What is liability?" She replied, "Anything I owed to pay outsider." I said to her, "It is nice to interact with you. Tomorrow, I will let you know about your selection." She replied, "Thank you very much." She left my home. Mary basic knowledge is very good. She should be the right person to get hired in my company. Next day I had send an email regarding joining my company. Fortunately, she had agreed to join my company. The email had my digital signature.

She had given her digital signature in the email. A special pen known as secript use for digital signature. Secript will help you to write in the email. On 27th August 2033 my earning had reached 700,000 dollars. I had gone with my parents to Plum restaurant. We had entered the restaurant. We were roaming along the restaurant to find a suitable place to sit. My eyes gaze at a girl who was standing in front of cake. It seems like today was her birthday. I had been visiting Plum restaurant for years in this day.

I had finally found my soul mate but we do not know each other. I had notice her staring at me. I had notice a teenager and I think it would be the girl's brother. A man asked, "Jack is that you?" I think he had seen me in the tv. I had nodded my head. The man proceeded towards my father and said, "I am Joseph Young." My dad said, "I am Jackal Café." Joseph, uncle said, "You must be Jack Café father. Meet my son Filipe and daughter Jacquelin." Dad had nodded his head. Joseph, uncle said, "I would request you, Jack and your wife to join my daughter birthday party." We nodded our head. We had joined the birthday party.

In this birthday party only seven members were their including us. After the birthday party I asked the girl, "What is your name?" She replied, "I am Jacquelin. Your name is hidden within my name." I had nodded my head. She had an oblong face. She is beautiful. Jacquelin do not know anything about her last birth. I asked her, "Jacquelin, where do you live?" She replied, "I live in Netherland. A month ago, my mom got transfer here." Joseph, uncle asked my dad, "Can we visit your home?"

My dad said, "Surely you can visit our home. When you are coming to our home?" Joseph's uncle asked, "Jackal can you share your number?" My dad had shared his number. We had left the place and proceeded our way to home. After reaching home dad had shared our location with Joseph Uncle. I secretly met my dad and said, "I had found my soul mate." He nodded his head as if he knew the future. Next day in the early afternoon we had greeted Jacquelin and her family.

My mom said, "Good afternoon Mr. and Mrs. Young. Mrs. Young may I know your name?" Mrs. Young said, "My name is Lillian Hannah before marriage now it is Lillian young. Is Jack your only son?" Mom said, "I have a daughter." Lillian's, aunt said, "Your daughter might had married someone." Mom said, "Yes." Lillian, aunt said, "I got transfer from Netherland to Washington DC. I am a Mechanical engineer." I asked Jacquelin, "Which school are you studying?"

She replied, "I studied in Whitewater High School. You are studying in which school?" I replied, "I am studying in Timber High School." In this way we talk for some more time. Her brother also studied in Whitewater High School. He is currently in 8th grade. They had studied in Vista High School before coming to USA. Next day we had visited Mr. Young home. The apartment consisted of 13th floors. They lived in 11th floor. I said to her, "I like your home." She replied, "Thank you and I like your home. Your programming skill is excellent. Did someone thought computer coding to you?"

I replied, "It is my natural talent and only family member know this secret." At that time Jacquelin was not that close to me. She said, "When time come you will say your secret to me." Jacquelin had visited my home on my birthday. I had ordered the cake online. The cake looks delicious from distance. My sister had also visited the birthday party with family. My nephews look so cute. I had introduced about Jacquelin to Alice. She and her family were happy to meet Jacquelin.

This time my birthday celebration took place in a club. The club's name was foothill club. The club was only 531 meters away from my home. I had invited only thirty people for my birthday celebration. I had planned to do Shakuntala show. I had proceeded towards a stage. I had picked up a mic after reaching the stage. I said, "I will be proving mathematically that the size of universe as calculated by our scientist is wrong. The size of universe is 93 billion light years. There are 2 trillion galaxies in this universe. The diameter available for galaxy is 65,761 light years. The scientist says the distance between two galaxy is one million light years. The size of galaxy ranges from 1'000 to 100'000 light year in diameter. So, it is very clear that the universe diameter needs to be at least 14 quadrillion light years. I strongly disagree the possibility of Big Bang to occur in past. Let us imaging an object to keep expanding. Everything inside the object will keep expanding. If universe is expanding then the atoms and molecule will also be expanding. If molecule and atoms are far apart within an object. There will be disbalance in order of object causing it to exist more towards gaseous state. Eventually all the object density will keep reducing. There is no chance for such universe to exist."

Everyone started clapping hand for me. I support both simulation theory and Vedic Rashmi Theory. I had press in my birthday. My speech was shown in news channel. I had return to my home with my family. Jacquelin was so impress with my speech that we had finally exchange each other phone number. In this stage we had become friends. In the Christmas she had visited my home. In this time, we had become close friends. I had bought a mini-Christmas tree for first time.

I had received a phone call from an unknown number. I had secretly gone to my room. Jacquelin and my sister had visited me during the Christmas. The phone conversation had went for few minutes. I had received a phone call from a Vedic scientist. They gave me an offer to visit Dehradun on 15th September 2034. I had agreed to visit them on 15th September 2034. At that time Jacquelin came inside my room. She asked, "Whom you were talking to?" I replied, "I was talking to Onam Khalsa. She is a Vedic scientist."

Jacquelin had a smiled in her face, "Vedic scientist are very inspiring. I am seeing father of interstellar travel within you." I nodded my head. I had given this good news to my family member. The new year party we had celebrated in a restaurant. I mean only me and Jacquelin had gone to have dinner together. Our parents started giving private time for us to understand each other feeling.

A Strong bond is formed from strong emotion attachment. The name of the restaurant was salt water. I had dance with Jacquelin after completing our dinner. I was dancing with a girl for first time. Let me name some song, love story, sorry, I am within you, etc. Together it seems to be best new year party we had. I am finding myself to hold some romantic relationship with Jacquelin. I had first time dated with her. I had told her that after three years, I will be shifting to a bungalow. She had express a desire to have living together relationship after three years.

After two years I had promised her to talk about this matter. That day onwards every weekend we go for dating. I won't be much focus on explaining every detail of our dating plan. On 10th April 2034 I had completed my high school study. I had decided to do BSC in physics. In this time Jacquelin had become my best friend. She had decided to do Computer Science Bachelor. By month of June, we got admission on the same colledge. I was admitted in Kennos Institute. Jacquelin had taken admission in the same institute. This institute was famous for paranormal activity courses.

Kennos provide many other courses in the field of law, management, tourism, chemistry, physics, computer etc. Kennos institute was constructed on the year 2000. The colledge had over 2000 books in the library. Jacquelin was living in my house. We use to sleep in the same room. There was no physical intimacy between us. On 1st July I had submitted an email stating the reason for taking leave on 15th September. After two days they had replied to my mail. I had got permission to take leave on 15th September to 15th November.

I had visited an online platform for getting my visa. I had receive my visa on 5th July. On 15th July 2034 Alice gave birth to a baby girl and was completely healthy. The baby is completely healthy. On 15th September I had reached New Delhi. I had boarded jet airways to reach India. I had come out of Jet airways. I had taken my luggage and came out of airport. I found a man waving his hand towards me. I had proceeded towards the man with luggage. I had check the timing, it was 12:55 PM. I asked him, "Sir, what is your name?" The man replied, "My name is Aditya Amrit. I will be guiding you in your journey." I asked Aditya, "What is your occupation?"

He replied, "I am a Vedic scientist from Dehradun. I will be telling the whole plan once we reached Imperial Hotel. The cost of this hotel is 180 Us dollar per day." I said, "I can easily afford to pay for this Hotel." My net worth at that time was 6 million US dollars. We sat on a taxi. Aditya Amrit was driving the car. I had immediately recognized that this car belongs to Aditya. I asked Aditya, "How far is the imperial Hotel?" He replied, "The hotel is around 14 kilometers from the airport."

Around half an hour later we had reached the Hotel. Aditya said, "I will come tomorrow to drop you in Delhi railway station." I had nodded my head. I asked him, "Will you go with me?" He replied, "I won't be coming with you. You will be going from Delhi to Dehradun. You have to manage your expense here." I had received 21,600 US dollar from them to come India. I had proceeded towards my hotel room. I have a plan to join Nasa as Rocket designer. I will be preparing for giving my interview in NASA.

I had been exempted from any written test. I had contacted NASA previously and came to know that they only want my basic rocket model. My luggage was carried by an employee in the hotel. I was impress with their service. I had never witness such an excellent service in cheaper price. After reaching my room, I had taken some rest. I was too tired of going out. I had ordered my lunch in my room. The best part was not having any additional fees in room service. These people prime focus is customer satisfaction.

I had called Jacquelin after having my lunch. We had spent some time in talking in phone. I had went out of Imperial Hotel next day. I had my breakfast before living the Imperial Hotel. Aditya was waiting for me out of the Imperial Hotel. The time was 9 AM. My train was at 10:30 AM. I had reached the station on right time. The train was on right time. I had taken an AC 2nd class train. I did not talk much with the local people. I do not know their language. I had reached Dehradun after three hours.

There was another person who was waiting in station. The woman said, "Good afternoon, sir My name is Chandni Shankar." I gave her a shake hand and said, "I am Jack Café." I followed her out of railway station. She had book a taxi for us. She sat next to driver seat. In India the driver seat is situated towards right side. Within fifteen minutes we had reached an ashram. This ashram is known to provide Vedic education. The name of ashram was Devananda Ashram.

I had use their bathroom in taking a bath again. This people have a rule that any visitor must take bath. My pathway to ashram was cover with flower. I was walking in bare foot. I had kept my shoe in their shoe rack. I had been greeted by ashram teacher and some student. A lady approached towards me and say, "Welcome Jack it is nice to meet you." I had immediately recognize it Onam Khalsa. I replied, "Onam ma'am it is nice to meet you." She replied, "Wow you can correctly recognize my voice. You are genius!"

I replied, "Thank you ma'am." I proceeded with a mic at the center of stage. Around a hundred student was there. I had given half an hour lecture on lucid dream. I had stayed in ashram over a month and had arrived to my home on 22nd October 2034. I had celebrated my birthday in that ashram. They gave me a special custard to eat. I had enjoy my birthday there. I had a work to hired chemist to manufacture more medicine. The moment I get my new Bangalow, whole responsibility would come to me.

Fortunately, Jacquelin had recruited ten chemists. I had to teach them to make my medicine. I had decided to invent a drone of my own. I had checked whether Jacquelin had recruited right people or not. Fortunately, she had recruited the right people according to the resume. She was in my room. I said to her, "I suggest you to pursue data scientist as your courier. I will be teaching you statistic once you graduate from your colledge." I had intentionally told this statement.

She replied, "You can teach me in my dream." I said, "You had pass my test and I will come to your dream to teach you." I had started going to colledge next day. I had informed recruited people that interview will be conducted on 10th November 2034. Ten people will be coming for the interview. I will be selecting the desire candidate. I had selected 6 people after conducting interview. I had rented a one room office to train them. I had started the training them on 20th November 2034.

The rented office was 75 kilometers from my home. It takes around 90 minutes to reach that place. I need to drop out from colledge on 21st November 2034 since work pressure was so much. Kennos Institute came to know that I am very busy now a days. They approached me to give me a fake colledge certificate. I had denied to have fake certificate from colledge. I have my own business so qualification does not matter. I am continuing learning the remaining course studies from my lucid dream.

My medicine does not allow you to visit someone dream for respecting others privacy. I can have infinite layers of dreams. There is no end in learning a subjects. I had continued my search for an agent.

I had found an agent on 22-12-2034. His name was Albert Handel. He had done his PHD in marketing. He had completed his PHD on 2028. At that time, he was 29 years old. He used to be Alice school mate. Alice had gave me his reference. Since he was my sister friend, I did not take any interview. We had decided to meet in a mall on 8th January 2035.

On 8th January I had gone to a mall. The name of the mall was Woodside. The Woodside mall was only 2.9 kilometers from my home. He told me that I need to visit KFC in Woodside. He wants to share my intelligence. He did not share his picture with me. As I entered the KFC there was so many people around me. I saw a man and said, "Albert nice to meet you." He replied, "Jack how did you recognize me?" I replied, "Everyone had pressed order and you did not place any order. You are wearing your cap reverse. There is a bag on the opposite side of your seat."

Albert said, "Wow! your sister was right you are genius. Jack, please take your seat." I had taken lucid dream help to identify Albert. I had seen a lucid dream yesterday of meeting Albert. I said, "I am currently training 6 people in manufacturing Ketasonide. The name of my medicine is Ketasonide. I had given them your contact detail. I have a request. Is it possible for you to help them establishing various franchise all around the world? They will train other people. Those train people will again train other people and it will go on."

Albert replied, "Jack your training strategy is on the right path. I will be teaching them International Marketing." I had given him a shake hand and proceeded out of the mall. I had used my private car to reach home. I had a confidential talk with Jacquelin. I said to her, "Can you recruit a data scientist?" She nodded her head. I replied, "I was joking. My HR will hire a data scientist for me." She said, "Have a nice day." I replied, "Thank you." I had immediately contacted my HR to hire a data scientist.

I told him to take the initial interview. The final interview will be taken by Jacquelin. I had soon discuss the same to Jacquelin. She asked me, "When the interview will take place?" I replied to her, "The interview will take place on 12th March 2035." My HR was able to recruit a data scientist on 12th February. She had given her HR interview on 22nd February. She was able to clear her HR interview. Her name was Carole Lewis. She was born in 11th February 2012. She had cleared her final interview with Jacquelin on 12th March 2035.

Albert had also completed his training with my employee. After few months Albert called me in my phone. He said, "India is your first foreign customer. So far, your business is spread across India, Sri Lanka and Bangladesh." I replied, "Thank you very much for informing. I like this progress." At that time my net worth had become 50 million us dollar. On 9th January 2036 my father had pass away.

My father did not had fortune of seeing my child or children. Few days before he looked completely normal. Doctor told he had died while having sleep paralysis. The report said he stayed in sleep paralysis for an hour before passing away. That day everyone cried and did not smile for next two days. I had an invitation to go London on 26th September 2036. I had passed this information to my family. They did not had any objection.

I had visited London on 26th September 2036. I had given a speech on lucid dream. People had understood the importance of lucid dream. At this time my product had spread across the world. My net worth had become 475 million dollars. I had return to my home on 1st October

2036. On 12th October 2036 Nasa had invited me for an interview of rocket designer post. Nasa had schedule my interview on 31st October 2036 at 9 AM. I did not go any security check up while entering NASA head quarter.

I had given my interview and the interviewer said after interviewing me, "The greatest illusionist had passed away 110 years ago." Another man proceeded towards me and said, "Sir, you need to wait in the waiting room for your result." My interviewer was a woman. I had followed the man. I had observed the man taking me to a dark room. I had proceeded inside the dark room and he attempted to push the door. I was quick enough to take my knife and stab in his stomach.

I had unfortunately lost my balance and had fallen down. The man attempted to close door before dying. My face was facing the floor. I had manage to get hold of door with my leg. I was pushing the door with my leg. I had manage to stay in this position for few minutes. I was able to open the door after his death. I had proceeded towards my interview room. One security had caught the woman who was taking my interview. She was one inch taller than me. The man whom I had stabbed pretended to be dead. The man stood more than six feet one inch.

The man would run away to hospital to cure his wound. Fortunately, my bodyguard would do a lie detector test on him. If he lies during the test, he will die. The same test will be implemented on this woman. My male bodyguard height is 226 cm and weight 306 kg. My female bodyguard height is 215 cm and weight 277 kg. My female bodyguard's name is Carole Saleem. Her date of birth is 9th October 2015. My male bodyguard's name is John Gazaway. His height is 226 cm 306 kg. His date of birth is 10th November 2015.

I had opened the digital lie detector. I had said to the woman, "Now you have to say the truth otherwise get ready to die." I asked her, "What is your name?" She replied, "My name is Elizabeth Gordon." I asked Elizabeth, "When you are born?" She replied, "I am born in 20th November 2012." I asked her, "Whom you work for?" She replied, "I work for you." At this point Carole thought she is lying. Fortunately, the lie detector did not show any sign of lie. I told Carole, "Elizabeth is telling the truth." At this time my phone ring.

I had picked up my phone, "Yes John." He said, "Sir Jonathan Colston says he work for you. There is no single mark for stabbing him. He had passed the lie detector test. How is this possible?" I replied, "Stay there with him. He has a fake bullet in his gun. The moment he fired the gun aiming towards your head pretend to die. He will be creating a situation of escaping from you." John said, "Yes sir." I had dropped the phone call. My bodyguards are trained to follow my command like robot.

I said to Carole, "Now Elizabeth will push me to the darkroom and I will get lock inside it. Elizabeth will say your game is over. A harmless smoke will be release. For some time, Elizabeth will be staying out. I will explain in detail to Carole and John once this acting gets over." I had gunpoint Elizabeth and had opened the door. Carole stayed in the room. I was passing though the dark room. Elizabeth suddenly snatches the gun and had shot me in head. She pushed me to the dark room and had pass away.

She ran towards the exit door and found my body guard there. She shot the bodyguard and ran away with Jonathan. A minute later they return back to office. My bodyguard woke up from fake death. Elizabeth opened the door and had called Carole. I had opened the dark room. We had gathered a secret place located under the ground. In this place everyone phone signal is nil. The reader is lost with no understanding of any event that had happened. Everett David wants me to kill me. He always wanted to be number one and cannot tolerate someone becoming more powerful than him.

The day I had started my international business he had started his plan. The day he had given me the offer of owning a bungalow, he was under my suspect. After starting my international business my actual plan had started. On 9th January 2035 I had again met Albert again for executing a secret plan. I had also predicted the future correctly that Everett David would execute his plan in killing me. I had told him to hire five special people. The reader would know the four people. Currently this four people are with me. The two-body guard was hired separately.

Today was the first time they were meeting Elizabeth and John. I had contacted NASA on 9th February 2035 to construct an under-ground House. I had explained to everyone about my plan in saving my life. My next aim to assassinate Everett David. I had explain the whole plan to everyone. Elizabeth will first inform to Everett David about my death.

Elizabeth informed Everett about my death and had decided to conduct a party on 1st December 2036. I said to Elizabeth, "On 1st December 2036 you should engage yourself with Everett. He should be very busy in the dance. He should be over dose with alcohol drinks. Then you should take him to a hotel room. I mean the party should take place in a hotel. After taking him to the room take the poison from your pocket and pour it in a glass of water."

Elizabeth said, "I will get caught after killing him. Please think of another idea." I asked her, "Is Everett David married or unmarried?" She replied, "He is married and it won't be easy to seduce him." I said to her, "Just become his personal assistant and leave rest of thing with me." I was staying in the hidden room. Next day Elizabeth had text the name of hotel. The name of hotel was Outlook Motel in New York city. I had shown the audio recording that Elizabeth showed me to NASA secret agency. They took another week time to verify that it is real.

In this one week they contacted the US government secretly. The government had decided to assassinate him secretly. Secret agency had connected the hotel manager secretly and had decided to kill him in heart attack. I had made a medicine that can cause heart attack after 4 days. The medicine will be given in his drink. I had secretly exported the medicine to secret agency of Nasa. They had exported to hotel manager. On 1st December 2036 he was in a hotel room with Elizabeth.

The poison was given to a drink which is known by her. Fortunately, he had consumed the right drink. He had enjoyed the party. Minutes later he left the room. He stayed fit for 3 days and suddenly had a heart attack. I had return to my home after his death. The forensic lab intentionally hid the main cause of his heart attack. The forensic people know about the secret assassination. I had told the truth to my family. The real reason behind Everett David dead was never known to media. I was selected as Rocket Designer for NASA on 12th January 2037. I had shifted with my family to Princeton New Jersey on 4th April 3037. Jacquelin will be staying with me.

She asked me, "Jack tell me how do we dream?" I said, "First let me explain what is conscious mind? Conscious mind is current state of awareness. Every activity you perceive before going to sleep comes under your conscious mind. At this time our conscious mind is active. Our conscious mind become deactive when we go to sleep. Unconscious mind is the part of consciousness that allow you to perceive dreams at night. Our dreams are decided by our subconscious mind. Our subconscious is so powerful and can seek information anywhere in this multiverse. It can also seek information from various timeline in multiverse. When our subconscious mind gets active it seeks information from parallel universe. Dream is just the simulated version of parallel universe event. The subconscious mind alters it according to its will. If our subconscious mind allows us to lucid dream, we get the free will to have lucid dream."

Jacquelin said, "Can you say something about F2L planet?" I replied, "F2L people are good in relationship. It is very difficult to get divorce in that country. If anybody partner had physical relationship with another person, in this case divorce can be granted. Under domestic violence divorce can be granted. The punishment is brutal in that planet. The way a criminal murder a person same way he or she get death sentence. I can't describe you in detail."

I had a dream a lucid dream on 5th September 2037. I saw a rocket design in front of my eye. I was able to see my electric rocket. Wow a great idea strike my mind. I had decided to wake up from my sleep. Jacquelin was sleeping next to me. Currently we are having casual physical relationship. After marriage we would have a serious relationship. I was studying working of alternate current from Nicola Tesla AC Model. I had completed my study last night. I had started to do an electric rocket design.

I had submitted my rocket design to NASA for review on 14th September. They had called me to explain about the rocket design. I had explained to them in detail. They gave me a month time for a better explanation. I had design a ppt for a better presentation. Finally, a month later my presentation got over. My rocket design was accepted. I had started working on the construction of the rocket. I had an information that Brent Stuart would be selected for Mars mission.

Space X had choose Alysha Carson. She will be going to Mars on 12th October 2039. My electric rocket can get charge by solar heat. I had completed my construction. I had completed in constructing rocket on 2nd September 2038. The problem was returning to Earth. I had also invented an inbuilt heat generator. I would to give some background about Brent Stuart. Brent Stuart was born on 7th February 2008 in Middletown. He had joined NASA on 2030. NASA was impressed by his performance and had decided to transfer Alysha to space X.

Elon musk had happily taken Alysha. She will be representing for space X. She was married after joining space X. I had requested NASA in training Brent Stuart. Nasa had accepted my request. I had started training him for Mars mission. The training went at its excellent pace. The rocket was launch on 7th April 2039. He was wearing a comfortable astronaut suit. The suit was orange color. There was an artificial gravity in the rocket. An astronaut needed to press a green button to start the rocket.

The direction of rocket needed to be manage manually. Only three people was going to Mars. Brent Stuart, me and Jacquelin. The reader would be surprise, why Jacquelin was going to Mars. I had told her to get training for Mars journey 18 months ago. It took me a month to convince Nasa the benefit of choosing Jacquelin. I had a dream to marry her once we reach Mars. Jacquelin had shown her interest in this proposal. The problem was how can we stay in Mars for such a long time.

I had thought to first land mars and return to Earth after 3 years. My rocket had a sleeping chamber. We have food for a year time. My rocket was not that advance as F2L planet. We can spend only a month in Mars. Jacquelin will be sending the data to NASA. A week later we spotted a creature who have a purple skin. The creature appears to walk in two legs. The creature approach towards in a friendly way. They had used a translating device.

The creature said, "Disconnect all your signal that will reach Earth." The creature was 2.2 meters tall. The creature was a female. She had a purple color skin, two horns and a thick tail. We were afraid to disobey her. The males might be huge in size. We did as per the instruction. She said, "Follow me." We followed her to an underground city. A huge male approach towards us and shot Brent Stuart. Surprisingly nothing happened to him. He shot the gun towards us.

Nothing happened to us. I had removed the oxygen marks and was able to breathe. Brent and Jacquelin had removed the marks. The huge male told, "My name is Agaoto Danan. I had injected oxycar in all of your body." I said, "I had contacted the Martian in my lucid dream and talked about my plan. The NASA scientist would know our plan if we did not disconnect our signal. We are dead in the eyes of NASA scientist." Jacquelin said, "Where would we go after 3 years?"

Agaoto replied, "You people would be sent to parallel universe. In that universe your parallel version died. You will be receiving back the signal in 5 minutes. My parallel person will be taking the dead body.

Jack you can continue your invention in that universe. My parallel version will vaporize the dead body. In that universe one in thousand women are every huge in size. The moment you reach the parallel world you all be of different size."

He told us to go inside a vertical chamber. We went inside the vertical chamber. We had lost our consciousness for few minutes. I have no idea of time period of staying unconscious. I had open my eyes and did not notice anything. The vertical chamber door was opened. Agaoto said, "Let me measure your people height." He scans our body with an AI laser. I was knowing this technology from F2L planet.

The AI scan can collect all your detail with a single scan. Agaoto said, "Mr. Jack you are 168 cm tall and weigh 63 kg. I am 242 cm tall and weigh 135 kg. Ms. Jacquelin you are 165 cm tall and weigh 60 kg. Brent you are 150 cm and weigh 45 kg. The detail of this universe you people should find out. We left the place and reconnected with NASA scientist. The NASA scientist was glad to connect back to us. We had bought Mars sand with us.

On 9th June 2040 we had landed in Earth. We had come out of rocket kept under quarantine for a week. Jacquelin and I were walking together. Brent Stuart was quarantine in a different room. I said to Jacquelin, "We do not know anything about this universe." She replied, "I do not know anything about this universe. We have only a week time." I replied, "Why don't we search online about our self." Jacquelin nodded her head.

Day 1 we spent time in knowing ourself from online source. I had completed my graduation from Kennos Institute. I had not make any medicine for lucid dream. I had not gone to any F2L planet. I was born on 22nd September 2016. My girlfriend was Jacquelin. Jacquelin was a biologist in this universe. The remaining days we spent time in social media post or chat for gathering more information about ourself. I had met with Jacquelin 3 years ago. It took around 6 months for her to be my girlfriend.

On 18th June 2040 we were release from quarantine center. Our house location was change in Washington DC. We went to our respective house. I live in a house but Jacquelin Parents live in an apartment. I was greeted by my sister. She was 170 cm tall and weigh 65 kg. She gave me a hug. My mom said from behind, "Jack it is nice to see you after months." I replied to mom, "It was nice to see you again". I and Jacquelin had removed the shoe. I had taken some time for freshen up. The washroom of this parallel universe looks completely different.

I had gone to my room. This room to looks so different from my universe. I still don't know about Alice married. She is 5 years older than me. I need to use lucid dream to know more about this universe. It took another 2 weeks to know about my past and present life. A month had passed for me to know past and present of this parallel universe.

My sister had married six years ago. She had married the same person in this universe. Jonathan Wells was five years elder to her. Only women are sumo-wrestler. They are huge in size. Their height ranges from 450 cm to 540 cm tall. In this parallel universe the definition of sumo wrestler is different.

The woman who are between 450 cm tall to 540 cm tall with a wide waist comes under category of sumo-wrestler. There is total 11 million sumo wrestler in this world. I had decided to see a new tv channel that exist in this universe. The channel name is Neual. It is about sumo wrestler show. The show happens in sumo camp. I had visited sumo camp on 3rd August 2040. I saw a sumo wrestler standing outside of entrance. She might be 456 cm tall. I had done a random estimate. She greeted me, "Good morning, Jack. Let me have a look at you." The whole world knew me.

She bended down and cradle lifted me. I had immediately thought of writing a researcher paper on quantum telescope. She said, "My duty is to hand over you to another sumo wrestler. You will be her toy." She carried me to 2nd floor's 3rd room. She pressed the calling bell. The door was opened by another sumo wrestler. She handover me to another sumo wrestler. The sumo wrestler said, "My name is Mary Taler." Mary placed me on her hip and closed the door.

Mary said, "I am 40 years old, 453 cm tall and weigh 1231 kg. I can run 4753 kilometer per hour. I can throw 615.5 tons 3119 meters away. My maximum lifting capacity is 326 kilotons. We have ability to control strength. I can hold egg without breaking it."

I was surprise to see the strength of sumo wrestler. They are like super heroines. She removed my shoe and kept it inside the shoe rack. She placed me on the bed. She said, "The sumo wrestler is above law. No sumo wrestler can go to jail at any condition. You will be with me for 2 hours. Normal person can stay for one hour. You are a famous person so you stay maximum 2 hours here. A sumo wrestler can marry another person. When a male sperm enters a sumo wrestler body it increases it size by 3 times within 3 hours. The bed is 141 cm tall; table is 220 cm tall; door is 600 cm tall and roof is 825 cm tall. I am married and have 3 children. My children are 2 boys and a girl. The girl will become sumo wrestler once she become 20 years. It takes only 40 days to become sumo. My children are 12 years boy, 9 years girl, 7 years boy."

I was appearing very small even after standing on the bed. Mary was very huge. Her waist diameter is 125 cm. Two humans can sit on anyone of her shoulders. She knees down. I was now coming to her forehead level. She sat on the bed. She was appearing taller than me even after sitting. I was almost coming to her neck level. She said, "I can maximum throw you 30,472 kilometers away." I was completely shock by her strength. I will be in asses in case she throws me that far. She placed me on her shoulder.

I had then sat on her hand. She had hip carried me. She had lifted me in one hand. I was like a toy to her. She had lifted me just holding my one leg. I had a horse ride on her back. I had left the sumo camp and had paid 20 dollars for visit. I had taken some rest after reaching home. I had started writing a thesis in quantum telescope. I had become 24 years old on 22nd September 2040. My birthday was celebrated on a club. I had given task to predict height of Sumo before her arrival. The door of club was 7 feet. The width of door was 3 feet. It does not have enough space for sumo to enter.

I told the people in my party, "Jeanne the sumo wrestler will be waiting out of club. Her full name is Jeanne Toribio. Her height will be 516 cm tall and weigh 1598 kg. Her age is 31 years old. She lives in Belleville." Everyone was shock to hear such accurate prediction. Everyone said, "Jack you are genius." Few minutes later Jeanne Toribio had arrived out of club. Jacquelin said, "Today you have to go with her. She is married." I replied, "This sumo can do whatever she wants." I had celebrated my birthday. The door was appearing so small in front Jeanne.

I had come out of door. Jeanne knee down lifted me up. I had a very nice view of roads. She said to me, "Happy birthday Jack. I will be taking you to my home. She placed me on her right shoulder and started to run. She took only 12 minutes to reach Belleville from Washington DC. She did not get tired in running so fast. I did not get scared. She opened her door with her personal house card. You can open any door of house using this card. She proceeded towards her room. It was 7 in evening. She said to me, "Tomorrow you will have dinner with your family." I nodded my head. She said to me, "I like obedient toy. You will be my toy for a day." Sumo wrestler tend to do less harm when they are not angry.

She placed me on her bed and said, "Jack let me get some water for you." Few minutes later she got a glass of water. I had drank a glass full of water. I asked her, "Have you drank water? My family member is in the other room." She replied, "Yes." She lifted me on her shoulder. She had started playing with me. Thirty minutes later she placed me on the floor. After sometimes she had used me as foot massage. She said, "Baby lay on my lap." I had lay on her lap. I appeared like a new born baby for her.

She placed me on the bed. She got down from the bed. She lifted me overhead with her right finger. She said, "Jack you weigh as a feature." She placed me on the bed. She showed me her recent family photo in her phone. Her mom was sitting on her left shoulder with her father. Her husband was sitting on her right shoulder. Her son was sitting on dad lap. She showed her teenage family photo to me. She had two siblings. She was the eldest among siblings. She had a 2 years younger brother, 4 years younger brother. Her parent and grandparent were there in photo.

She said to me, "My mom is 492 cm tall. In this photo she was carrying 6 people. I was sitting on my mom left shoulder. My two years younger brother was sitting with me. My grandparents were sitting on her right shoulder. My four years younger brother was sitting on her right hip and dad on her left hip. Jack you will have your dinner. I had my dinner and had gone to sleep an hour later. I was sleeping on Jeanne stomach. I can jump on her stomach and she won't feel anything.

I had woke up at 7 AM. I had got down from her stomach. Jeanne said, "Good morning, Jack. I will spend some time with my family." I replied to her, "Good morning, Jeanne." She came back to the room on 8 AM. She had helped me doing the morning daily routine. I had my breakfast and took an hour rest. Jeanne placed her one finger under my chin and had lifted me to her eyes level. It was very easy for her to kill me. She flipped me in such a way that I had land on the bed.

She knees down and held me in one hand. She had gently placed me down. She said to me, "Kiss my knee baby." I had kiss her knee. She had lifted me up and gave me kiss on my cheek. She had placed me down. She lay down on bed facing towards the pillow. I had lay down on her body. After an hour she told me, "Jack now gets up from my back." I got up from her back. I sat on left arm. She placed me on the bed. She had placed me on her right shoulder. She said to me, "My total lifespan is 422 years." I replied, "You appear very young."

She said to me, "Now it is time to have the lunch." We had our lunch shortly. We took an hour rest. She threw me up to touch the roof. She lifted me in one finger. She had spined in one finger. I had lost my sense. I had gain my senses after one hour. She lifted me upside down. I was scared. She had safely placed me down. She had lifted in one finger. She had threw me up and half flip me and placed her one hand on my back and another on stomach. She attempted to throw me on the bed. I had caught her arm.

She had placed me on her hip. She had lifted me up just holding back side of neck. I was moving my legs in air. She placed me on her right shoulder and dropped me to my home. We had waved hand on each other. I had pressed the calling bell. Jacquelin had opened the door. She had gave me a kiss. She said, "I thought you are gone forever. It is impossible for me to snatch you from a sumo wrestler." I said to her, "In this parallel universe anything can happen to me. It is better not to resist any sumo wrestler." I had entered inside my house and Jacquelin had closed the door.

I had published my thesis on quantum telescope on 18th April 2041. That day Jacquelin parents and her brother had visited my home. Mr. Joseph said, "Mr. Jack we would like to fixed a date for engagement." I replied, "I think 6th June 2041 would be an ideal date for engagement." Everyone had agreed to the date suggested by me. Jacquelin, parents had stayed in our home for few days. On 2nd June my sister and her family had visited my home. Other relative of my side had visited my home.

My home was decorated with red balloons. I and Jacquelin had sat on a swing. The swing slowly moved up. The lights were completely focus on us. I had taken a ring from my suit and placed it on Jacquelin middle finger of right hand. Jacquelin did the same thing to me. Our guest had really enjoy the party. I had received the invitation from NASA after a week. I have to give a lecture in NASA. I have to reach NASA on 2nd August 2041. I had inform my family about the good news. I had started working on my presentation.

I will be demonstrating working of quantum telescope in a computer simulation. We can see things from very far distance. With the help of quantum telescope a satellite in Andromeda Galaxy would be visible. Quantum telescope can be magnified maximum up to 10^{22} times. An object that is 10^{22} kilometer away might appear to be a kilometer away in quantum telescope. We can also reduce its magnifying power.

On 2nd August 2041 I had reached NASA on right time. I had entered a hall and found scientist from different parts of the world. I had successfully given my lecture about quantum telescope. Everyone understood my explanation. I had left the hall and entered inside my car. I was driving my own car. I was stop by a sumo wrestler on my way back to home. She is 537 cm tall. I do not know her name. She lifted me of the car and started running. Within 42 minutes we reached Las Vegas.

She was placing me on her left shoulder. She said, "My name is Felicita Matlock. I am born on 13th March 2015." She opened her house door and entered inside her house. She has a card to unlock her home door. She had taken me to her bed room. I was surprise to see Jacquelin. She went to washroom to freshen me up. I asked her, "Where did you do your education?" I was sitting on her bed with Jacquelin. She was sitting beside me. She replied, "We were have a separate school and colledge for sumo wrestler. I had set a real game for both of you. The name of game is maze runner trap. You would be asked to complete a maze. You have to complete the maze without getting stuck. The whole game will be happening in virtual world but if you get stuck a sumo wrestler will kill you. You will be directly teleported to Ukanio Frenfinin home. You will see yourself in same height in the F2L planet."

Jacquelin asked, "Why are you putting us in danger?" The sumo did not answered her question She carried us and laid us down in two different chambers. I had instantly found myself near a huge maze. I had notice Jacquelin in same place. "We need to find the right path out of this maze. If we cross this maze successfully, we would go to F2L planet." Jacquelin asked, "What will happen if we get trap by sumo wrestler."

I replied, "The moment we get caught by sumo wrestler she would kill us. In real world poisonous gas would be release inside the chamber. We will died in virtual and real world. If we cross the maze our sleep chamber would be teleported to F2L planet." She asked, "How do you know?" I replied, "I had seen this maze in my lucid dream and know about the outcomes. There are people who want to kill us. I won't say you the reason. It can create a paradox." She nodded her head.

We followed the right path to complete the maze. It took only four minutes to complete the maze. We lost our consciousness and woke up inside a sleeping chamber. Ukanio lifted me of the sleeping chamber. Ukanio was 322 cm tall and weigh 238 kg. I had observed Uyakuniko also lifting Jacquelin from sleeping chamber. Uyakuniko was 315 cm tall and weigh 228 kg.

I had use telepathic technique in knowing our death trap. They came out of lab room and placed us in bedroom. Uyakuniko said, "Jack and Jacquelin welcome to F2L planet. We kept you inside the sleeping chamber for 2 Earth weeks. Our research had shown that you had visited the same planet in parallel universe. In this universe everyone owns a sleeping chamber. Everyone can do researcher about any planet in virtual sleeping chamber. My occupation is electric engineer. Ukanio occupation is teleportation station operator."

I said to Ukanio, "This room appear different than the parallel version." Ukanio said, "Thanks for saying something new. I just know you had visited parallel version of F2L planet. You and Jacquelin are declared dead in Earth." I asked to him in surprise, "Why my telepathic technique could not catch it?" Ukanio said, "Our plan is beyond any genius in Earth. We had hacked your lucid dream. You have to complete all your invention in 21 Earth years from beginning. You cannot go out of this apartment. With the help of sleeping chamber, you can go anywhere virtually. This is a secret mission done by us. Only our family know that you have come to F2L planet. Everyday 2 Earth hour you will be left alone to spend time with Jacquelin. All the facility to build new device will be given. Another person knows about your visit in F2L planet. I have hire Corie Belar to take care of you and Jacquelin. She is only 21 F2L years old and today is her first day. After 14 Earth years Uyakuniko will make a test tube baby from you and Jacquelin. Once the child is born, he or she will be given to a person as orphanage. The people will know the baby birth as synthetic life of Earth people. After 21 Earth year your physical body age will be 28 years old. All the device that is helping you and Jacquelin to stay alive will stop working. Your child will be safe in this planet."

Corie Belar entered the room. She was 327 cm tall and weigh 256 kg. We had introduced ourself to her. She had told us about herself. Corie said to us, "It is nice to meet a genius scientist and his wife." I was the genius scientist mentioned by Corie Belar. I have 252 months in my hand. I had re- invented Ketasonide after 2 years. I had 228 months left in my hand to complete all my invention. Ketasonide will help you to lucid dream. You can enter into other person dreams only to know their dream and send message. You cannot change their dream.

You also have power to stop people in entering your dream. You can do anything in your lucid dream. I had invented a quantum telescope after 22 months. I had 206 months left in my hand to complete all my invention. The quantum telescope is much powerful than a normal telescope. The maximum magnification power is 10^{23} times. An object that is 10^{23} kilometers away would appeared 1 kilometer away in this quantum telescope. I had invented a quantum telescope after 16 months that can view the present of far away object. I had 190 months left in my hand to complete all my invention.

This special quantum telescope will emit tachyon particle to catch the present scenario of far way object. A tachyon particle exists in information state. So, this particle can travel infinite speed as mass of this particle is 0. I had invented a new device after 33 months. This device can help us breathe any air across the whole universe. I had 157 months left in my hand to complete all my invention. I had invented another new device after 33 months. This device can convert any unsuitable climate suitable to us.

This device will generally create an invisible layer out of your body. It will be stopping all sort of heat exposure and freezing temperature. You can stand on sun without feeling its heat. I had 124 months left in my hand to complete all my invention. I had invented a new device after 16 months. This device can help us to change our form. You can disguised into any creature in this universe. I had 108 months left in my hand to complete all my invention. Ukanio called a doctor to his home after 24 months.

The doctor had taken my sperm and Jacquelin ovum. We were left alone after taking our sperm and ovum. Jacquelin asked to me, "Will we really died after 84 months?" I replied, "When time comes you will know everything." I don't want to reveal the biggest suspense of future. I had invented a stargate after 33 months. This was my last invention. The stargate had the facility of time traveling, travel any where in this universe and visit multiple parallel universe.

If a person need to time travel he or she need to achieve negative density. If matter in our body is replace with antimatter we can travel backward in time. We can travel in future with our matter form. The time between entering the stargate and existing out will never be known. Since we exist in information state while travelling inside stargate.

Contents